WHISPERS OF SUMMER

Whispers of Summer

ROWENA KONG

Summer Novel

Contents

Prologue

"When Suddenly Becomes A Lifetime..."

She slowly repeated the title of a pocket book her hand un-
knowingly rested on while clearing out the cluttered den in
her three-year-old apartment. One of the old cupboards was
packed with books of various sizes and thicknesses—they
were her most treasured belongings that she did not dare to
part with and this upcoming Christmas was the perfect time
to provide some cleanup for her precious treasures. She came
up with the idea of sending them to the book-cleaning store
that had just opened last week and was conveniently located
about two blocks down the street. She considered herself
blessed to have discovered it in spite of the lack of ads and
publicity, which the humble store literally could not afford.
Thus, it was time to bless its elderly owner with the service
that she had been hoping to receive. Not to mention, today
was the perfect day to send over a dozen boxes of hefty
books—she could not take more than three days off from her
newly-landed job, which unfortunately meant that she was
unable to return to her hometown to spend Christmas with
her parents this year.

Picking up the quaint-looking novel, she peered closer to
study the picture on its cover—it was in the centre of the bottom half of the book—a grayscale photograph of an empty,

wooden photo frame, sitting on a desk with writing and signa-
tures scribbled all over its surface. The frame's grimy glass
cover slightly out of place, and the writing on the desk was so
small that it was impossible to read, so she didn't bother to
decipher it. She refused to read the back cover due to an insa-
tiable desire to discover the story within its ancient pages. It
did not appear as if it were a romance novel, but who knows?
She refused to judge a book by an ambiguous cover....

Chapter 1: A Wish Granted

"Ugh! No cake with candles to blow out, no gifts wrapped in pretty wrapping paper, and not a single photo with friends or family!" A young woman could be heard muttering to herself as she made her way to the nearby park. She looked to be around her late twenties, with dark brown hair tied into a messy bun and a youthful face that was wearing an expression of slight frustration. Her outfit consisted of a flower-printed white blouse underneath a light pink sweater, along with a cream-colored pencil skirt and dark brown heels. She continued muttering as she flopped on to one of the stone benches and kicked off her shoes. She bent down and picked them up, placing them next to her.

"But it's still my birthday... What a style—twenty-first century solitude," she grumbled bitterly. The young woman sighed and stared listlessly at the fountain in front of her, which was currently silent. Her eyes flicked to the clock tower that was in the center, noting that it was now a quarter 'til midnight. Her dreary mood sank even lower as she looked around—the surrounding sidewalks and streets were completely devoid of people. She sighed again and blinked back the tears that were starting to build. She had been pressured to work another (underpaid) overtime tonight, but she hadn't complained; after all, *someone* had to do it. She lifted her eyes to the dark sky overhead, noting with dissatisfaction that there were patches of clouds scattered about. She let out a third sigh, this one deeper and longer than the ones before. Her lips curved into a bittersweet smile and she shook her head. "Look at you, Trinna Summer. Always putting others before yourself. No wonder you're such a workaholic!"

She glanced up at the sky again and murmured, "I'm sorry I missed your sunset earlier, dearest Father. But then can I at least have some bright stars?" She clasped her hands, bowed her head, and closed her eyes, as if hoping this small prayer would help to bring out the stars that she so desperately wished to see.

After a minute of silence had passed, Trinna opened her eyes and looked up at the dark sky hopefully, but to her dismay, there were still no stars. Indeed, it seemed the clouds were mocking her and had become bigger and darker instead, as if intending to make sure that her wish was not granted. She bit her bottom lip and blinked rapidly—tears had been threatening to come again—before huffing in annoyance and crossing her arms defiantly.

"Fine, then I'll just sit here and wait. I don't care how long it takes—I'm not leaving until I see at least *one* star!" she declared aloud. Please, she thought. Just one is all I ask for. I only need one to make my "free" birthday wish. She let out another sigh and shook her head lightly to banish the negative thoughts that were scattered around in her mind. She knew she was being stubborn and unreasonable, but a stressful day at work was always bound to cause such a change in her mood.

Deciding to kill some time, she dug inside her purse and pulled out a pocket-sized novel. She glanced around, and a frown appeared on her young face upon noticing that the area was not very illuminated. She reached inside and took out her phone, opting to use its flashlight as the light source instead. With her book in her lap and one of her hands holding her phone-turned-flashlight, she soon found herself absorbed in the novel as she patiently awaited her "miracle"...

All was quiet and peaceful, without a single soul in sight, when a young man suddenly appeared on the path leading to the fountain. He looked to be in his late twenties or early thirties, with short, dark brown hair and a handsome face. He was wearing a light blue dress shirt underneath a brown leather jacket, along with black dress pants and black dress shoes. In one hand, he carried what appeared to be a large brown paper bag, which he now raised to eye-level to give it a slightly disappointed look.

"You're my very first creation... Do you know how much courage it took for me to turn you into a reality? But now I'm alone and there's no one to share you with... Danson Loveland, you are pathetic," he mumbled, shaking his head and releasing a small sigh as he continued making his way towards the nearest bench facing the fountain.

Upon realizing that he was not alone in the park, he stopped short of walking any closer. He was slightly stunned that he didn't even see her until she was practically right in front of him, but he supposed he had been too lost in his thoughts to pay attention. Resigning himself to sit on the other end of the bench, he gave a light, awkward cough and walked back a bit before sitting down. He set the bag down next to him, and out of curiosity, stole a glance at the young woman. So absorbed was she in the pages of her small novel, however, that she seemed to be completely unaware of his presence. He looked away quickly, not wanting to be caught staring. Though the situation was slightly awkward, he decided not to think about it for now.

In contrast to the state of rapt attention the young woman was giving to her novel (which he secretly thought was endearing), Danson found himself overwhelmed by the serenity of his surroundings: the utter silence, the lush greenery, and the scent of fresh mint. He was especially taken with the flora—such a sight was rare to come across in his residential area, and although it took some imagination on his part to visualize the correct shades of color, he was incredibly delighted at the drastic change of scenery the park provided, despite the surrounding darkness.

So enthralled was he by the tranquility of the atmosphere that he found that his eyelids had begun to droop a little. He wasn't extremely tired, but his short time in the ambiance had helped soothe him greatly, and he found that all he wanted to do was to bask in the peace for a little while longer. It was moments like this that reminded him that he needed to stop and enjoy life's simple treasures every once in a while. The thought brought a small smile to his face as he closed his eyes and whispered a quick prayer of thanks to the Heavenly Father above.

A small cry suddenly broke the silence, followed by a loud sniff. His eyes snapped open and he turned to his left, towards the origin of the sound.

Trinna was sobbing uncontrollably—she had just reached the climax of the story, and the protagonist's unspoken suffering was too much for her heart to bear. Adding to the character's anguish was her own sense of loneliness, and as the very reminder sprung back into her mind, more tears came flowing forth. Unable to stand it any longer, she flung her book and phone away from her and buried her face in her hands as she continued to cry.

Needless to say, Danson was very shocked...and very concerned. Her items had landed on the ground not too far from where he sat, and without a second thought, he bent down and picked them up. He gave the book several quick pats to get rid of any dirt that might have gotten on it, and then examined her phone to see if it had been damaged (and thankfully it hadn't). He spared another worried glance in her direction before slowly getting up from his seat and approaching her cautiously.

"Hey, Miss... Are you okay?" he asked hesitantly, trying his best not to sound too forward.

His soft voice abruptly startled her out of her thoughts, reminding her that she was actually still sitting in the park. Had she been *that* engrossed in the novel? Apparently she had, for she had not been aware of another's presence. How long had he been here? She raised her head so quickly, it was a miracle she didn't give herself whiplash. Her tear-stained face, however, only served to worry Danson even more.

Trinna found that she could not respond to his question, partially because she wasn't sure how to answer, and partially because she was mortified that he had caught her in such a vulnerable state. Danson only continued to gaze at her quietly, unsure of whether he ought to take another step forward or maintain his distance.

They stared at each other in silence for a few more seconds before her gaze landed on the novel and phone in his hands. The sudden glimpse of the book caused her to choke up once more, and as the events in the book came rushing back to the forefront of her mind, she could not stop the second wave of tears that surged forth. She dropped her head back into her hands and wept bitterly, her body slightly shaking from all the emotion she was releasing.

Danson was now thoroughly alarmed and looked around nervously, now wondering if he needed to call the authorities to let them know that there was an emotionally unstable young lady in the park at this time of night. Despite the lack of people around, he didn't want to attract unnecessary or suspicious attention...and a young lady crying her heart out was bound to create such a scene, which would only be made worse by his presence. Moreover, it was nearing midnight; he really needed to get home (and he was sure that she did as well).

However, a strange feeling had aroused within his heart the moment he had laid eyes on her young face—he didn't know why, but seeing (and hearing) her sob so wretchedly was tugging at his heartstrings, and even though she was a complete stranger, he felt a strong desire to comfort her. His mind was telling him that the young woman was possibly trying to trick him, but his heart was telling him otherwise...

So what happened next was out of instinct more than anything else.

Danson placed the book and phone next to her sobbing frame, took a seat next to her, and in the next instant, wrapped his arms around her, giving her a hug. He expected her to push him away, but surprisingly, she didn't. Other than a slight stiffening of her form, she made no other sign that she was opposed to his sudden gesture, and even snuggled slightly closer to him. He began to gently pat her on the upper back, and because he wasn't sure what to say (and he didn't want to offend her by saying the wrong thing). With her head now nestled on his shoulder, he also realized that the scent of mint he had detected earlier came not from any of the surrounding plants or flowers, but from her perfume.

If someone had happened to stumble upon such an intimate scene at that moment, Danson honestly wasn't sure how he would have reacted. It was already strange enough that he was comforting a young woman who was completely unknown to him, yet even more bizarre was that such an act did not make him uncomfortable in the least. And if the fact that she was still clinging tightly to him was any indication, it seemed that she did not find their current situation awkward either.

They stayed that way for a few minutes, until the deep chime of the clock tower from the fountain alerted them to the fact that it was now midnight.

Trinna, who had finally stopped crying and could now breathe more easily, suddenly became aware of her situation and pulled out of the embrace slowly. Apart from feeling extremely shy, however, she found it odd that there was no additional reaction of embarrassment...at least for now.

"I'm so—"

"Are y—"

They had spoken up simultaneously, and upon meeting his intense (yet worried) gaze, Trinna found herself speechless. She turned away slightly, grateful for the darkness that concealed the light blush that now dusted her cheeks. As she raised her hand to wipe away any remaining tears, she felt a soft nudge to her shoulder. She turned back around to see him offering her a tissue, which she gladly accepted. After wiping her eyes, she hesitantly looked back up at him. "Thank you," she whispered meekly.

"You're welcome," he murmured in response. He was relieved that she was feeling much better than before, and to hide the small smile that was tugging at the corners of his lips, he cast his eyes up to the sky...only to have his mouth nearly drop open in shock. "Wow... What a sight...."

Out of curiosity, she looked over at him, wondering what could have provoked a response so filled with wonder. He caught her gaze and pointed to the sky, the barest hint of a smile on his face. She followed his instruction and gasped in astonishment upon seeing the marvelous sight that greeted her: numerous stars twinkling merrily, bathing the sky in silver brilliance, and not a single cloud was in sight. Trinna felt like she was going to cry all over again, only out of sheer joy this time. She jumped up excitedly and ran towards the fountain a bit, stretched her arms out to her sides, and spun around in a circle, laughing as she did so. She stood there for a moment after she stopped spinning, waiting for her dizziness to pass. Tilting her face upwards and closing her eyes, she whispered a quick prayer of thanks to the Lord above for granting her wish. Once finished, she returned to sit back down on the bench.

She looked over at the young man, who had been patiently waiting for her to finish her little "celebration." She noticed that one of his hands was now clutching a brown paper bag, and because she was naturally curious, she pointed to it. "What's that?"

Danson smiled at her and gave a slight nod towards the splendor above them. "Such a majestic sight... It's the first time I've seen so many stars at one time in a single night, and even though it is not scientifically possible for all twelve zodiac constellations to be seen at one time, I feel as if bits of each of them are all here right now," he stated quietly, giving the scene another quick glance. He turned back towards her, his head tilted slightly as he asked, "And judging by your reaction minutes ago, I presume that you had been waiting for their appearance?" At her timid nod, he reached into the bag and pulled out a box. "I've been wanting to share this treat with someone, but could not find anyone...until now," he expressed honestly, his eyes gazing down at the "package" before him. His voice was soft, but there was a sad undertone to it that affected her in a way she could not explain. He looked up at her—Trinna swore she had never seen a pair of eyes as mesmerizing as his—and continued in the same soft tone, "Would you be so kind as to help me fulfill this humble wish?" He gave her a small, hopeful smile.

"It would be my pleasure," she responded automatically, offering him a warm smile of her own. It was the least she could do since he had taken the time to try and comfort her a while ago.

Danson's smile widened at her answer, and without further hesitation, he opened the box. Trinna let out a small gasp of surprise. Inside the box was a custard cheesecake, baked to perfection and beautifully decorated. However, one corner of the cake particularly caught her eye instantly—a miniature fairy tale-style castle that had been meticulously sculpted out of icing. So accurate were the details that it seemed as if someone had shrunk the popular landmark itself and placed it on to the cake.

"This is amazing!" She exclaimed, finally tearing her gaze away from the delicious treat. She looked at him with something akin to admiration and gave him a broad smile. "Did *you* make this? It's gorgeous! It honestly looks too beautiful to eat!" Realizing that she was nearly shouting, she ducked her head in embarrassment and cleared her throat before returning her gaze back to him and continuing in a much quieter tone, "You have been blessed with a gift. Such talent..." she trailed off, not knowing what else to say. Unable to hold his gaze any longer, she went back to staring fascinatedly at the miniature castle perched on top of the cake.

Danson could only stare at her in silent gratitude. Ever since finishing the cake a little more than an hour ago, he had been hoping to hear some sort of praise from anyone, even if it was just a simple "Good job!" However, the chef that he was training under was strict and seemingly unfeeling, and the students were not much better. He had honestly considered throwing the entire thing in the trash, but something had stopped him. And now, hearing such honest praise from such a simple young lady (of whom he knew nothing about)...

That unfamiliar sensation within his heart was roused again, leaving him to wonder...

Just who was this girl?

Chapter 2: An Unexpected Gesture

Trinna threw away the covers with such force that they landed in a pitiful pile on the floor of her bedroom. Sunshine had been streaming through her lacy white curtains for quite some time now, gracing (or perhaps disturbing) her weekend slumber with soothing warmth, accompanied by the brilliant light that flooded the entire room. She had thought that she could enjoy her weekend in the same manner as always: relaxed and free of any disturbance. However, it seemed that this day would be different.

She had first woken fifteen minutes ago to the sound of her doorbell ringing. Hoping that the unwanted visitor would give up and go away if she did not answer the door, she attempted to go back to sleep...but to no avail. Whoever was at the door was incredibly persistent, and after fifteen minutes of sleeplessness, she decided she should probably answer it, lest the neighbors start complaining...or she start screaming.

With a frustrated sigh (and a few unladylike swears), she forced herself out of bed and grabbed her pink sweater robe that had been knocked to the floor as well. She hurriedly put it on and stifled a yawn as she kicked her covers aside, grumbling under her breath all the while. She stomped her way out of the bedroom and towards the front door, intent on giving whoever was on the other side a piece of her mind...

...Only to be slightly taken aback. She rubbed her eyes, partially to get rid of any remaining sleep, and partially because she couldn't quite believe who was standing outside the door. At the young man's bright smile, she found her initial rage slowly giving way to a dull irritation, and she plastered on a meek smile of her own. Though she was still upset, she hid it well.

"Good morning, Miss 'Summer'! I am really sorry for coming so unexpectedly.... How are you today?" he greeted all too cheerfully.

She cursed herself inwardly for not being more properly dressed and pulled the robe tighter around her body as she replied evenly, "Good morning, Steven. I'm doing well, thank you. This is indeed unexpected.... It's only eight..." she narrowed her eyes ever so slightly at the last statement, knowing that her 'visitor' knew full well that she was not to be bothered during the weekend...least of all in the mornings.

Steven was not bothered by the warning, however, and only nodded in understanding. "I know, and I am *terribly* sorry to have woken you up... But please trust me Trinna, it's different this time!"

She could only gape at him in confusion. "What on earth do you mean? I know you are the company's most hardworking courier delivery guy, and Saturdays are no exception... But it still doesn't make sense for you to come to *me*, as I am not on duty. There should be someone else in charge back at the receiving department, right? Have you come to the wrong door? Not only that, but I just finished another overtime yesterday and there's my privacy to consider—"

Steven raised a hand and waved it dismissively, effectively cutting off her rambling. His smile became wider as he presented her with an elegantly-wrapped package. "I know spring has just begun, but I feel that there's a hint of summer in the air, especially for you, 'Big Sister' Trinna!" He added the endearment in hopes of softening her demeanor more.

Trinna was even more confused as she stared at the package. "Wait...what? So this isn't for the company, so I'm not signing for it on the company's behalf...?"

Steven could only chuckle at her innocence. "Miss Trinna...'Summer', can you not feel it? I could already tell from the wrapping paper that it's a birthday gift, for you! You kept your birthday a secret from everyone in the company ever since you started there.... Why torture yourself like that? That's why this," he waved at the package, "*had* to be delivered by this morning, and that's why I came here, even though I knew I risked facing your wrath by waking you up so early."

Trinna remained unamused and raised an eyebrow in skepticism. She glanced at the package and then shook her head with a sigh, fighting back her temper as she asked her next question in a calm voice. "If it's for me personally, then why did it go through you and the company? I can see the address, Mr. Steven Song."

Steven blinked, and then looked at the package himself, confirming her thoughts. "Well," he said slowly, "this *is* the company's address, that's true... But the intended recipient really *is* you—it has your name on it!" He glanced at another label. "And let me see, the sender is 'Danson Taylor Loveland...'" he trailed off uncomfortably. He could tell she was getting annoyed and he prayed to whatever deity was listening that he would not be on the receiving end of her fury.

Trinna rolled her eyes and scoffed, "Right. 'Danson Taylor Loveland'. You might as well say 'Danson Taylor Love' or something..."

Just as Steven shook his head, however, Trinna's eyes widened with realization. "Wait...Wait a second. Did you say

'Danson Taylor Loveland'?" she asked him, her expression now one of pure surprise.

"Or 'Danson Taylor Love'?" he countered submissively, unsure of what she was getting at.

Her mouth formed a small "o" of surprise before she hurried away from the door, leaving him standing there in utter confusion as he watched her grab a pocket novel from the inside of her purse that was lying on the couch. He was even more bewildered as he watched her flip frantically through the pages and give the book a few good shakes.

Concerned that the lack of sleep may have somehow negatively affected her, he called out, "Trinna, is everything okay? What are you looking for?"

The young woman sighed and seemed to be talking to herself as her visitor looked on in concern. "I lost it—the business card that I was using as a bookmark. That must be how he obtained the company's address...."

***

After a slice of cheesecake had been set before each of them—he had fortunately stopped by the general store after the class was over to buy a pack of paper plates and box of plasticware—they had started chatting for a while. After exchanging introductions, she had surprisingly disclosed the reason for her breakdown: the emotional attachment to the novel she had been reading and the sense of loneliness she had felt on her birthday (which had now passed). She had apologized for causing him so much trouble and then thanked him profusely for his kindness.

He had merely smiled in return and said that it was nothing, ignoring the small voice in his head that had been snickering in amusement. He had been a little stunned that she had opened herself up so easily to a complete stranger. Was it possible that she too, had felt something...? As soon as the thought crossed his mind, however, he quickly dismissed it. Nonsense!

A ridiculous idea! Perhaps she was just an open person who talked to anyone about anything, provided she was given a listening ear. Yes, that must be it. And yet, as he had watched her take another bite out of her slice of cake, he still couldn't take his mind off of the scenario from earlier—his gesture had been instantaneous and her response had been acquiescent.... It had felt so natural....

She had not stayed for very long, stating that she was tired after a long day at work. He had insisted on walking her home, but she refused the offer, saying that he had already done enough. Being the gentleman that he was, he had persisted, pointing out that it really wasn't safe for a young woman to be out on the streets during this time of night. Only when she told him that she had already put in a request for a cab to pick her up did he relent. He still wasn't very comfortable with the idea, but had been unable to say anything else before she had quickly gotten up from her seat, slung her bag over her shoulder, and thanked him again for his kindness (and the cake) before taking off.

He had been left staring after her, a mix of thoughts and emotions tumbling around in his mind and heart. He slowly packed up the cake and then arose from his seat to throw his (untouched) slice in the nearest trashcan. As he had been walking back to the bench, his eyes swept over the ground around the area, making sure that no large crumbs had been left behind. While peering under the bench, however, a flash of white caught his eye. Curious, he reached for the object.

"What's this?" he had asked himself in a whisper. He could tell there was print on the small card, but was unable to read it due to the surrounding darkness. He quickly pulled out his phone from his pocket and turned on its flashlight.

It had looked to be a business card, with a company's name and address printed on it. Trinna's name and contact information was also listed. Danson ran a finger over her name, his brow creased in thought.

"Trinna Doreen Summer... Hmm...." he hummed quietly as he looked at the address for a few seconds longer, an idea forming in his head....

***

After Steven left, Trinna walked slowly over to the coffee table and placed the surprise package on its glass surface before taking a seat on the couch. She stared at it for a few minutes, her heart pounding in anticipation. She was still trying to grasp the fact that *he* had sent her a birthday present. Had he felt sorry for her after her admission and done it out of obligation? Or was he just trying to be nice? She honestly didn't know what to think of his surprise gesture, but she decided to put it out of her mind for now. With trembling hands, she reached out and slowly began to unwrap the gift, taking the greatest care not to rip the beautiful wrapping paper. She opened the box and after peering inside, reached in and pulled out the unknown object.

Slightly amused, she looked at what she pulled out of the box. "What's this? A rather cute, pink plastic cupcake with a candle-shaped lightbulb... Does he see me as a child?" she mused aloud as she turned the 'gift' around. However, a small button on the opposite side of the "candle" caught her attention.

" 'Press And Blow Me'? Haha, okay then!" Trinna smiled and followed the instruction, pressing the button while simultaneously blowing out the "candle."

To her amazement, the cupcake split apart and transformed itself from the inside out, revealing a velvet mint flower so intricately woven that it seemed as if someone had placed the actual flower itself inside the clever contraption. She let out a breath she wasn't aware she had been holding, and as she inhaled deeply to replenish the oxygen that her lungs had been deprived of for those few precious seconds, she caught a whiff of the scent that was radiating from the flower—a scent that was all too familiar to her, since she wore it as her perfume every day.

"Happy Birthday. I know this is a little late, but I still hope that I am the first to know..." Danson's smooth voice was coming in the form of a recorded message, from inside the center of the "flower," upon which sat a figurine of a sleeping angel.

A slight dampness on her cheek startled Trinna; she hadn't even realized she had started tearing. She brushed away the tear with a slender hand and as she raised her eyes from the gift, she realized that there was still an accompanying birthday card. She quickly set the gift down and reached over to grab the card, which had a picture of a beautiful canvas painting of an enchanting style castle on the front. He had modeled his miniature icing fairy tale castle on his last night's custard cheesecake after it. She opened the card eagerly to read the message inside:

I hope you will like this card with a scenic painting of a fairy tale castle, (a reminder of last night's creation) as there are still a few more hours remaining before Friday ends in the Western part of the country. We on the East coast are too far ahead.... Therefore, I hope you are able to enjoy your birthday to the fullest extent because it is still not too late.

When I arrived home in the early hours of the morning (and I trust that you arrived home safely as well?), the first thing I did was to plant a few roses and carnations on my apartment balcony...such beauty is simply nonexistent in the place where I live. It is the first time in my life that I have done something like this, and I feel that it is a sign of something special, though of what I am not exactly certain. Perhaps it is the fact that knowing a monotonous situation can be changed, and with change comes positive expectations...

Thus, I hope you will find a reason to be happy amidst the storms of life. Remember, there is always sunshine—and perhaps even a rainbow—after every storm.

Thank you so much for your company last night; it was a pleasure to get to know you.

Danson (Taylor) Loveland

Trinna was so moved that she could once again feel tears threatening to spill over. A very strange feeling had stirred within her heart, but she couldn't figure out what it was. She could also feel her cheeks suffusing with warmth as memories of the night before came rushing back in startling clarity, to a point where she could almost *feel* his arms around her again....

She let out a yelp, shaking her head violently to get rid of the memory. With a red face and racing heart, she took several deep breaths to calm herself down. After she was certain that her cheeks had returned to their normal color and her heart had slowed down to a more normal rate, she leaned her back against the couch and simply stared at the gift and card.

Her mind was buzzing with questions, but she couldn't answer any of them. The only thing she knew was that he had suddenly appeared at the moment when she thought she was at her loneliest. Was this a sign that there was something more to come? She had never been a big believer in fate or destiny, but something in her heart told her that this hadn't been just a random occurrence....

Chapter 3: An Uncertain Coincidence

Having spent the past thirty minutes browsing through the entire literature section of the store, Danson Taylor looked up from the shelf of books he had been skimming through and sighed softly. His morning had passed by quite uneventfully, and while he didn't mind the quiet, he was starting to become a little bored. He was a little surprised that despite his lack of rest from the night before—he had been unable to fall asleep after returning home—he was not tired. He had only been a little more sluggish that morning, which quickly disappeared after having his usual cup of morning coffee. He absentmindedly noted the time on his wristwatch before nodding to himself and then taking out his phone.

He opened the application for the regional courier service and quickly navigated to the appropriate page, smiling when he saw that his expedited package had been successfully delivered and signed for receipt. Even though he couldn't picture her exact response, he hoped she had been pleasantly surprised. At the very thought, an unexpected warmth blossomed from within his heart, causing him to pause momentarily in bemusement. How strange. He had definitely never experienced such a feeling before, yet it was not unpleasant—there was a peculiar fondness to it that only made his smile become a little wider as he moved to put his phone back in his pocket.

The device suddenly started chiming a classical tune, and a quick glance at the screen told him that it was his assistant.

"Good morning Simon!" he greeted enthusiastically. "What's up?" He knew he must have sounded a little too joyful, but thankfully, Simon didn't seem to question it.

"Good morning to you too, Dan!" Simon responded in an equally cheerful tone. Danson smiled at the nickname.

"I called because one of our research participants did not give his consent for us to use his videotaped session after being debriefed. So we complied with his request and took out the video," Simon explained, hoping this information would not suddenly ruin his boss's good mood. He found the young man's new behavior both extremely refreshing and slightly perplexing, but he didn't want to push his luck by asking for the reason behind the change.

"I see," Danson responded, his tone becoming slightly more serious as he contemplated the situation. "So we'll have to exclude his data from the study's analysis later." He shrugged, but then remembered that his assistant couldn't see the gesture. He quickly added, "Oh well, there's nothing we can do about that."

"Leslie and I are still looking for participants, so hopefully we'll have more data soon," added Simon. It was good that Danson wasn't bothered by the news; however, that also meant that they would need to work harder on the study. Back at the office, he wrote down a few notes and nodded to himself. "Anyways, that was all that I wanted to tell you, Dan. Nothing else has come up so far, so let's hope this goes well. Enjoy your weekend, and don't worry, we'll take care of it."

Danson smiled and nodded in understanding. "I know you guys will, but seriously, if you need any help, don't hesitate to call me. Thanks for letting me know of the situation. Don't work too hard; you need to enjoy the weekend too." He heard Simon laugh on the other end of the line before saying that there was more work that needed to be done, so he had to go. They exchanged goodbyes and Danson hung up, slipping his phone back into his pocket.

He started making his way out of the store, partially because none of the latest publications there interested him, and partially because he had apparently caught the attention of a group of college-aged girls. They had been darting conspicuous glances at him for the past ten minutes or so, whispering and giggling all the while. Feeling slightly embarrassed for being the subject of their attention, he quickly hurried out of the store. He zipped up his leather jacket as a gust of wind blew past, and looked up to glare at the deceiving sunshine—despite its presence, it was still quite chilly outside, and the occasional wind only made it worse. He decided to head to the main library, which was only a few blocks away. He walked quickly, not wanting to spend any more time outside than was necessary.

A blast of warm air greeted him as soon as he entered the building, which made him sigh in relief. He gave the librarian a polite nod and smile, and was about to head towards his usual section of the library (General Science and Psychology) to see if he could find any new publications on neuroscience, but then hesitated. As if some unknown force was guiding him, he turned around and headed back towards the staircase. He climbed the stairs and reached the second floor, where the Contemporary Literature section was located.

He had no clue what drew him there, but he figured a change in routine wouldn't hurt. He wandered to the first aisle and began looking at the titles, running his finger along the arranged line of materials on one of the shelves. He was unimpressed and was about to move to another shelf when a particular title caught his attention.

"When Suddenly Becomes A Lifetime, Volume 2," he murmured. Giving a slight shove to the surrounding books on the right, he carefully pulled the smaller novel out from its place on the shelf and quickly flipped through the crisp pages. Something about this book was vaguely familiar...

He studied its plain cover and the title again, and suddenly, realization dawned on him. His brow furrowed as he questioned uncertainly, "Wasn't she reading this at the park last night?"

Chapter 4: A Second Meeting

Seeking the second volume of a 20-year-old novel series, When Suddenly Becomes A Lifetime, by Edwise K (official pen name). Any secondhand volume is acceptable. Compensation is negotiable. Contact details listed below...

Trinna stuck some more tape around the notice, ensuring its permanent position on the bulletin board at the park. She stepped back and admired her handiwork before giving a small nod of her head and putting the roll of tape back into her backpack. Picking up two bags of groceries, which also contained other miscellaneous items, she started to make her way to the opposite end of the park.

She must have read the first volume of the series for the thirtieth time, and yet her eyes still gave way to tears upon each reading. She was all too ready to get her hands on the next installment, since the first volume had given her a few unexpected plot twists and some exciting cliffhangers. Even though she had gotten the book for free at one of the neighborhood book exchange stations located on her college campus during her last semester at university, she hadn't had a chance to read it until much later in the year, after she had landed her first (and current) job. In a way, she was almost quite glad that she had been unable to return home to spend Christmas with her parents last year—ever since she first flipped through those worn pages, she hadn't been able to put the book back down. As a consequence, she now carried it with her wherever she went, and if she had some spare time, she would find herself lost in the world that the author had created. She supposed that her own personal circumstances had helped form her emotional attachment to the story.

The day was a beautiful one, albeit chilly. However, with the sun already shining at its brightest, Trinna found that she did not mind the cold at all. With the addition of fresh, cool air, she found her thoughts drifting away from the novel and focusing on the colorful flowers that were still in bloom, as well as the soon-to-be flowers that were currently still buds. The garden was maintained extremely well, and she found herself smiling at the thought of returning again soon, just to take in the beauty of God's work. As she passed by the fountain with the clock tower, she suddenly paused as memories from the night before (or early morning, as the case may be) flashed back into her mind. As if on cue, the clock started to chime and Trinna looked up to see that it was noon. Warmth immediately rushed to her cheeks as he crept back into her memories...

"Twelve hours ago... It seems as if it was less than twelve seconds ago," she whispered to herself, shaking her head to clear her mind. She continued on her way, but at a much slower pace as she took in the breathtaking sight before her: yellow and white wild daisies dotted the emerald-green grass like a small patchwork quilt. Trinna found herself so taken with the sight that she set her bags down to allow herself a moment of rest to enjoy the view even longer. She glanced down and her eyes landed on a dandelion that had grown right next to the walkway on which she had been strolling.

She crouched down and gently plucked the wild plant from its spot and smiled. "Mom once told me a story of a little girl whose wish came true after blowing you like a candle. May I try as well?"

As if the dandelion had given her its permission, a cool, sweet breeze suddenly blew past, tussling Trinna's dark tresses playfully. She pursed her lips and blew lightly, watching in childlike wonder as the ball of "fluff" dissipated and the seeds danced above her other outstretched palm before disappearing into the air.

"Thank you..." she murmured, a small smile on her face. She pulled herself back into a standing position and leaned down to pick up her two bags.

A sudden wail behind her caused her to whip quickly around in concern, her bags almost slipping out of her hands as she did so. She found herself facing a crying little girl, who was pointing an accusing finger at her, along with a young woman whom she assumed to be the girl's mother. Trinna blinked in bewilderment—the little girl was blubbering over the sad fate of the "poor helpless dandelion," and the mother was doing a poor job (in her opinion) of comforting the daughter. A part of her wanted to explain the situation to the crying child, but her common sense was telling her that such an act would be useless; the child would not be able to understand her anyways, so why waste the time? She resisted the urge to sigh in exasperation as she turned around to continue on her way....

"Little sister, please don't cry anymore. Here, a bright pink rose! It's much prettier than a small dandelion, don't you think so?" a warm voice suddenly spoke up, causing the girl to stop her crying momentarily.

Trinna froze and whipped back around, her eyes widening in shock. That voice... It couldn't be!

Sure enough, Danson Taylor Loveland approached the pair from behind, holding out a pink rose in one hand. He looked like he was holding something behind his back as well, but from her viewpoint, Trinna couldn't tell what it was. She watched as he knelt down in front of the little girl, who happily accepted the pretty flower from the handsome stranger and said a shy "thank you". To her utmost confusion, Danson smiled and returned the sentiment, glancing briefly in her direction as he did so.

The mother gave him her thanks as well, and after a quick apology to Trinna for the trouble, the pair bade their goodbyes went on their way. An awkward silence descended upon the remaining pair as Trinna found herself at a loss for words. She had not expected to see him again, much less twelve hours later at nearly the exact same spot as their first meeting.

Danson gazed at her quietly for a moment before taking a cautious step towards her. She didn't protest, so he took that as an encouragement and walked up to her, a small smile on his face.

"I bought that a few minutes ago from the flower cart lady at the entrance. A little spontaneous of me, I must admit. I hope you don't mind, but it still comes with this." He withdrew his hand from behind his back, revealing a pink balloon tied with a gold ribbon. It had been a little challenging to keep it hidden from the little girl, but upon seeing the surprised look on Trinna's face, he decided it was worth it.

Startled at the sudden gesture, she blinked before letting out a small giggle. "Oh! No wonder you looked a little...odd."

Danson smiled as he reached into one of his pockets and pulled out a black marker. He uncapped it, and quickly drew a sketch of a smiling doe-eyed bunny before handing the balloon over to the young woman. And as he watched her face brighten into the same expression she had worn when she had seen his cake, he felt that odd warmth in his chest again....

Chapter 5: An Honest Conversation

"It's lovely! Thank you so much!" Trinna exclaimed as she accepted the small "gift" from him, her smile bright enough to rival the sun itself.

Danson was relieved that she did not seem to mind losing the rose—it was originally meant for her, but his inner gentleman had pressured him into giving it to the crying little girl who had just left. However, upon seeing the smile on her face as she gazed at the ballon, he couldn't help but form a small smile of his own. As he watched her finger the gold, satin ribbon delicately, he guessed that she must have had a fondness for ribbons. He didn't know why, but he hoped this little discovery was right. He made note of this minute detail and stored it away in his mind for future reference.

Now carrying a surprise gift on her person, Trinna found herself in a slight predicament as she tried her best to hold on to the balloon with one hand, while trying to hold on to her groceries with the other. Danson quickly noticed her struggling, and felt slightly guilty about the additional inconvenience he had indirectly placed on her.

He held out one of his hands and gave her a warm smile. "Those bags look rather heavy for you; would you like some help?" he offered kindly.

Trinna stopped struggling for a moment and turned to look at him. The minute they locked eyes, however, any protest she may have had died on her lips. Her momentary state of dumbness caused her to loosen her grip on one of the grocery bags, which promptly dropped on to the ground between them. Her eyes widened in surprise and she could feel the heat rushing to her face. She immediately turned her head to hide her blush, praying that he hadn't seen.

However, Danson was oblivious to her telltale sign of nervousness, and instead was more interested in the fallen bag, which had opened to reveal its contents. His curiosity piqued, he quickly bent over and picked up the bag.

"You're into baking as well?" he asked, his tone laced with both delight and surprise. His smile had grown even wider at the prospect of finding someone who held the same interest as he.

With her head still turned away, Trinna slowly released a deep breath as she forced herself to calm down. Once she was certain that her face had returned to its normal color, she turned back around and faced him with regained composure. She put on a false smile and replied, "Oh no, I don't really do it often. It's just...just that..." she trailed off uncertainly.

Danson waited patiently for her answer, not knowing that his earnest expression was only causing the poor girl in front of him to become even more tongue-tied. He too, entertained the idea of attending a baking class for the sake of satisfying one's curiosity and attempting something new and different.

Trinna mentally cursed herself for her lack of coherence and tried again, "I...er...wanted to try my hand at that custard cheesecake," she admitted sheepishly, cringing at her own honest (but stupid) answer.

Danson's expression brightened even more as he remained blissfully unaware of the girl's self-consciousness. "Really? You mean that custard cheesecake from last night, right?" He was intrigued that a simple dessert seemed to be her source of motivation.

His voice suddenly took on a boyish tone, making him sound so excited that Trinna was uncertain of how she should answer his question without embarrassing herself even more. So she gave a simple nod of her head in affirmation.

He chuckled lightly as he lifted the bag of baking accessories and ingredients. "Is this your first try?" he asked gently, his voice reverting back to its normal softness.

"Well...yeah," she replied lamely. Even though her outward appearance seemed calm, she was mentally throwing a fit—how could this guy, whom she had only met twelve hours before, render her so speechless? It was if he could read her mind! (Though his mesmerizing eyes and velvety voice weren't helping matters either).

A shy smile appeared on his face and he rubbbed the back of his neck sheepishly. "I'm sorry, I didn't mean to be so straightforward. But I could just tell from your answer..." he trailed off and glanced away, choosing to look inside the bag again.

Finding resistance futile, Trinna decided to give in and offer an explanation. "It's all right. It's just that... That custard cheesecake tasted just like the one I had for the first time aboard a plane a long, long time ago. I honestly thought I would never get a second chance to experience that 'once-in-a-lifetime' flavour again..." she smiled and sighed happily as the memory of that first custard cheesecake came to mind, momentarily forgetting about the handsome young man standing before her.

Danson stood quite still, his head tilted to the side as he listened to her explanation. He was struck by how open and honest she was—the fact that a simple dessert could hold so much meaning for her... It was quite extraordinary. He allowed her a moment of silence before clearing his throat to catch her attention. Once she had snapped out of her reverie, he began to speak, although not without some hesitance.

"If I too, can be honest... Last night was my first attempt at baking a cake. And not only that, I even altered my instructor's recipe, so he did not give me any credit for either the 'custard cheesecake' assignment...or for my first class," he said quietly, grimacing slightly as he did so. In hindsight, perhaps it had not been the best idea, but he didn't regret it. Still, failing the first assignment and class...

He was startled out of his negative thoughts by an indignant gasp, the source being none other than the young lady standing before him. Trinna shook her head in disbelief. "How could he do such a thing?! That's terrible! But don't worry, I would definitely give you ten stars for that custard cheesecake! It's definitely the work of a professional chef, trust me!" She paused for a moment to catch her breath, before continuing in a much softer voice, "Not to mention, that cake saved my day...or rather, my night...." She looked at him and gave him a soft smile, her cheeks coloring slightly upon her admission. She turned her head away, not only out of embarrassment, but also to escape his piercing gaze.

Danson could only stare at her in wonder. Her words had not only raised his mood tremendously, but they had also caused that same peculiar feeling from the night before to stir within his heart. Something about her was special of that he was sure. Her very presence caused his heart to flutter—something that had never happened before with any of the previous girls he had met. Not only that, but to meet her twice in twelve hours... Was it fate or destiny? Or was it just pure coincidence? It appeared that they were meant to cross each other's paths at just the right place and time, such that even obstacles (if there were any) couldn't hinder them. Many questions had arisen, but none of them could be answered for now. However, one thing was for certain: Trinna Summer had entered his life for a reason...and he would find out what that reason was.

Chapter 6: A Long-Awaited Answer

"That's right, Mom! I'm gonna learn how to make that custard cheesecake—the same one that we had on the plane so many years ago when we went overseas for the first time as dad's anniversary gift to you, in the form of our most memorable vacation! Ah, the sweetness of it! I can't even describe how I felt when I had it earlier!" Trinna's words came out in an excited rush as she spoke to her mother over the phone. Seated on the couch in her living room, she stopped to catch her breath and could only grin as she heard her mother chuckle.

Mrs Summer smiled. It had been a while since she had heard Trinna sound so happy, though she slightly suspected that a simple custard cheesecake wasn't the only reason behind her daughter's exuberance. Hearing Trinna so excited, however, made her happy as well. So she could only exclaim in response, "That's wonderful, dear! Indeed, it's been such a long time since we've had that special treat; I absolutely cannot wait for you to share it with us! Of course, it will have to wait until I'm done with my spring cleaning and gardening," she paused for a moment and then continued in a hushed voice, "And I'll keep it a secret between us for now, otherwise your father might start nagging me day and night, and then I won't be able to get anything done around the house..." she trailed off and then a mischievous smile started to form on her face, something she was glad that Trinna couldn't see. "So...from whom, or where, did you get this mysterious recipe, dear? I promise I won't tell anyone."

Upon hearing her mother's question, Trinna suddenly found that her mind had gone completely blank. Her eyes widened and she stuttered, "Umm, well...er, about that, Mom.... I..."

Mrs Summer raised an eyebrow at her daughter's sudden lack of coherence, but her mischievous smile had now turned into a sly grin. A-ha! Her daughter was definitely hiding something. Of course, that was a sign that as her mother, she now needed to press for more information. Choosing her words carefully, she spoke in the most casual tone she could muster, "Such a rare recipe...surely it must've been very expensive to buy." Mrs Summer smirked as she waited patiently for her daughter's answer. Depending on how Trinna answered this question, she might be able to gain a little more information.

Trinna bit her bottom lip nervously, wondering whether she should play along and answer her mother's question, or find a different topic to divert her attention.

Before she could respond, however, she heard her father proudly declaring in the background that the leaky faucet on the kitchen sink had been fixed. On the other end of the line, her mother heaved a great sigh of relief—Trinna mentally mirrored her mother's response—before saying regretfully that she needed to go, since the dishes had been sitting in the sink for over an hour and needed to be washed immediately. All too eager to avoid her mother's further questioning, Trinna quickly ended their conversation, and the two of them hung up.

As Trinna replaced the handset back on its stand, she let out a deep sigh of relief. That was close! She grabbed a nearby pillow and hugged it tightly, her lips forming a silent prayer of thanks to her Heavenly Father above for helping her "escape" from the awkward situation.

She leaned back and raised her hands to massage her temples lightly. Her thoughts wandered back to everything that had happened during the day, causing a small smile to form on her face, as well as a slight blush to her cheeks. Danson—after a quick explanation on the situation with his name the night before, she had settled on addressing him by his "first" given name—had been kind enough to carry the heavy baking supplies for her, all the way back to her apartment. However, when she invited him inside, he had politely declined, stating that he didn't want to invade her privacy, especially since they were only acquaintances thus far. He didn't want to cause her any extra trouble or arouse suspicion among her neighbours. So Trinna had bade him farewell and watched as he left. His kind mannerisms, along with his polite demeanor, further confirmed her opinion that he was a respectful and refined young gentleman—no doubt quite a catch among those of the opposite gender.

As she was thinking, Trinna's gaze fell on the pair of books that were resting near the side of the transparent glass coffee table. She felt her smile become a little wider (and her cheeks a little redder) as a particular memory surfaced....

After Danson had taken her grocery bags from her, they had decided to take a stroll around the park, since the day was perfect for such an activity. They had chatted for a while, bouncing from topic to topic. At one point, his surprise birthday gift for her had also come up, and for some strange reason, she had been compelled to reveal the reason behind her liking for mint flowers; and in return, he had given her the long-awaited answer to a question that had been haunting her for years.

As they started to walk out of the park, Danson had suddenly stopped. Trinna stopped as well, and had watched in mild surprise as he fished out a pocketbook novel from seemingly out of nowhere and then turned to her with a small smile. He held the book out towards her. "Here. For you."

"Wha—" she had started to say, but then abruptly cut off when she spied the title of the miniature-sized novel. Her eyes immediately widened and she gasped. "Ohmygosh! The second volume of When Suddenly Becomes A Lifetime!" I've been looking for a copy of this book for the longest time, but I could never find it!" she exclaimed excitedly. She had started to reach out for it, but then hesitated, pulling her hand back a little. She looked up at him shyly. "How.. Where did you find this?" To say she was shocked would've been a massive understatement—her mind was still trying to process the fact that the book she had been searching for had finally been found, and in his hands, no less!

Amused by her response, Danson gave a slight chuckle. "I checked it out from the main library not too long ago. I recognized the title from the same novel you were reading last night, and was a little curious. But then I saw your signs..." He had let the rest of his sentence remain unsaid, but his intention was clear. He smiled warmly and motioned for her to take the book.

She had been stunned speechless, which only caused the ensuing silence to become awkward once again. Danson had started to wonder whether he was being way too forward with her—after all, they had only just met over twelve hours ago—and was about to retract his offer, but before he could say anything, she had reached out and gently plucked the small book out of his hand.

She had flipped through the pages, backwards and forwards, before shutting it and hugging it close to her chest. She looked up at him, her eyes bright and her lips curved into the softest smile. "Thank you," she whispered reverently.

Danson had smiled back, his heart once again filled with the inexplicable warmth that he had already experienced twice earlier that day. "You're welcome. This volume is out of print for more than ten years. It's no wonder you have not been able to obtain it from the stores. For some reason, it is a limited edition volume which was sold for less than a year before it was pulled off the book market. That I have no idea why...It's strange," he replied gently.

Lost in the memory, Trinna let out a small giggle and sighed dreamily. "Definitely not a random occurrence, but definitely more than a coincidence as well...How mysterious," she murmured quietly to herself.

Her eyes glanced away from the books and landed on the wrapping paper that was used to wrap the gift that had been delivered earlier that morning. She gasped, her eyes widening with realization, "Oh my goodness, I forgot to thank him for this gift! Ugh! Trinna, you silly girl! How could you be so absent-minded??"

She shook her head and continued muttering to herself as she picked up the wrapping paper, but the delivery slip (which was still attached) suddenly caught her eye. She peered closer at the handwriting, her brow furrowing in thought. "The signature... Why does it look so familiar? Is my mind playing tricks on me again?"

She frowned, trying to remember where she had seen the familiar script. Her hand seemed to move of its own accord, and she found herself picking up her used volume of When Suddenly Becomes A Lifetime, Volume 1. She flipped through its pages until she reached the back cover. Her eyes only scanned over the last page for a few seconds before dropped open in shock. She blinked rapidly before looking up from the page to the delivery slip and back to the page again, making sure her eyes weren't deceiving her. They weren't.

Because right there on the last page, was a miniature copy of Danson's signature. His was among a dozen others, paired with what seemed to be a farewell message to a Japanese exchange student who had studied at the same university that she had attended.

Trinna felt like her heart had skipped a beat. She could only sit there in disbelief as her mind tried to process the fact that once again, fate seemed to have a hand in both of their lives. Was this a sign that something greater was in store for both of them?

***

In another apartment complex, a young man was lying on his bed, his arms folded behind his head as he stared up at the ceiling. Though his outer appearance was relaxed, his mind was the complete opposite—the day's events had been continuously replaying, like a song stuck on repeat. It was now an hour past dinnertime, and he had eaten considerably less tonight than usual. Normally, he would be searching up journal articles on his computer around this time, but tonight was different...

He didn't know how, but they had started talking...and he was enjoying it. They hadn't really talked about anything in particular, choosing instead to converse about several different topics. Watching her as she spoke about everything so freely and continuously.... He hadn't been able to keep himself from smiling as he listened to her, and he had noticed that when it was his turn to speak, she gave him her full attention, and would always respond with a comment or two of her own.

Somewhere along the way, he had become curious about her thoughts over his gift from that morning, so after they had fallen into a peaceful silence, he decided to ask, "So...um, did you like the gift from this morning?" He winced slightly, hoping he hadn't sounded too desperate. He stopped walking and turned to face her, waiting for her response.

He had watched as her face lit up and a big grin appeared on her face. She nodded vigorously, her words coming out in a rush, "Oh my goodness, yes! I absolutely love it! At first I thought it was a little childish—I mean, a pink plastic cupcake with the light bulb shaped as a candle? But then I pressed the button, and oh my gosh, I was so surprised! The flower is absolutely lovely—I can't believe it smells just like my favorite perfume! And the sleeping angel inside... Simply amazing! And the message—" Having realized that she was rambling (and out of breath), Trinna abruptly stopped talking and lowered her eyes bashfully, not wanting to look him in the eye after such an embarrassing display. She pretended to be fascinated by the cover of the book he had let her borrow.

Danson, however, had only smiled. Seeing her become so excited over what he thought was a simple gift made him inexplicably happy... as well as causing that strange warmth in his chest to return. He had noticed that in her rush, she had forgotten to thank him, but strangely enough, he did not mind in the least.

"Actually," she said suddenly in a soft voice, "the mint flower is one of the most meaningful things to me in the world." She had kept her eyes lowered, her unexpected confession surprising both him and herself.

"Oh? And why is that?" he inquired, his head tilted to the side in curiosity.

She had smiled at him lightly before responding, her words coming out in the same soft voice. "It happened when I was still a young girl in elementary school. My grandma was extremely sick and had been hospitalised. My parents were devastated—it was the first time I had ever seen them cry," she hesitated briefly, and Danson could see that she was trying to hold back tears herself. He resisted the urge to hug her, the same gesture of comfort he had offered her the night before. (Where this urge even came from, he did not know).

Trinna sniffed a little before continuing, "I felt so helpless, so not knowing what else to do, I ran off to the hospital's chapel and cried until I fell asleep," she paused again and took a deep breath before continuing, "I ended up spending the entire night there, and I was awoken before dawn by a mysterious voice, whispering to me that everything would be all right and asking me for the meaning of a certain thing in particular. I know it sounds silly, but I swear that's what happened. Of course, I was a little disturbed, thinking that someone was trying to pull a prank on me. I got up from the pew I fell asleep on and looked around, but the only thing I saw was a bouquet of mint flowers on the pew behind me. The next thing I knew, my mother was running towards me, laughing and crying. My disappearance had worried her greatly, and after I assured her that I was okay, she told me the good news—my grandma had been moved from the intensive care unit to a general in-patient room..." she stopped for a moment and wiped her eyes, before turning to him and giving him a small smile. "To this day, I think that the bouquet of mint flowers was God's way of saying that he saw my family's tears and heard our cries and prayers."

Danson had been astounded. Not only had he been moved to tears by her story, but there was also something else that he suddenly remembered. He had given her a gentle smile and asked in soft voice, "Did you know that the symbolic meaning of mint is 'protection from illness'?"

Trinna gasped in surprise. "No, I didn't know that at all! You're the first one to tell me this. I think...I think this is the answer to that mysterious question all those years ago! I've always wondered... But no, it makes sense now." Eyes brimming with gratitude, she had given him another smile and bowed her head slightly. "Thank you... Thank you so much," she murmured.

Danson blinked. While lost in the memory, something else had been nagging at him. He got up from his bed and walked over to his desk, on which his laptop was placed. After waiting for it to take a few minutes to start up, he accessed his Internet browser and clicked on one of the pages he had bookmarked. He scrolled through an alphabetical list of flower names and then stopped when he reached the second half of the page.

Mint – Protection from illness; Virtue; Warmth of feeling

" 'Warmth of feeling'..." Danson repeated quietly to himself. He stared at the screen for a few seconds longer before closing out of the window and shutting down his laptop. He ambled back to his bed and resumed his previous position, his mind now racing faster than ever as particular events from earlier in the day surged forward:

The mysterious warmth in his chest that had blossomed after seeing that his package had been delivered... And after she had seen the balloon... After he had given her the book... And again after he had heard her reaction to his surprise gift.

And even now, as he continued to stare at his ceiling, he could feel that strange sensation (though not as intensely). And yet, it wasn't bothersome; on the contrary, it made him feel quite content, as if he knew that everything was all right. He let a small smile appear on his face before closing his eyes and drifting off to sleep.

To be continued.....

www.ingramcontent.com/pod-product-compliance
Lightning Source LLC
Chambersburg PA
CBHW070943120726
47908CB00005BA/1505